CW00411521

Drefan
and the
Knucker Dragon.

Book One

D.J.Williamson

Illustrations by

Emma Martin

**A Renweard Press
Publication.**

First published in the UK in 2017
Copyright © 2017 David Williamson
Illustrations Copyright © 2017 Emma Martin
Renweard Press Logo Copyright © 2017 Jillian Robinson

1

ISBN: 978-1977625137

Renweard Press, Worthing,
West Sussex. UK

email: renweardpress@yahoo.com

Drefan
and the
Knucker Dragon

Chapter One

In the year 550, there lived a young Saxon boy by the name of Drefan. He came from a small hamlet called Hamm Tun, which was in the Kingdom of the South Saxons on the southern coast of Englaland, and he lived there with his father who was also called Drefan, his Mother Wilona and his younger sister Ellette. Hamm Tun, which meant 'the hamlet by the water meadow', was positioned on a rise of land close enough to a stream so that they could easily fetch water, but not so close that it would flood if the stream overflowed its banks in the wet season.

He and his family lived with twenty or so other families who were led by their tribal elder, Eldwyn the Brave. Each family lived in their own house which had walls built from wood with a dirt floor and thatched roofing made from straw. Eldwyn the Brave as village Elder, lived in a slightly larger house known as The Hall, and this was also the place where the Hamm Tun Council would meet.

Their houses were oblong in shape; they did not have any windows as we know them, just small triangular shaped holes cut into the woodwork which were known as 'wind eyes' to let in a little light and air. Everyone in the family, sometimes including animals, shared the one space where they ate, slept, cooked, brewed beer and sat and spoke with friends.

Each home had a small hole in the centre of the roof which let some of the smoke escape from the fires that burnt night and day, although during the summer months, the fires were moved outside when the weather was fine enough. It was on these fires that all their food was cooked, usually in a large earthenware pot, though bread, which was flat and round, was baked over hot stones placed within the embers. In the winter months, the fire was also their only source of heating and everyone would sleep around it trying to keep themselves warm. As there were no chimneys, all the houses were very smoky and a fine layer of soot covered everything within.

Life for these Saxon folk was very hard but the people were content to live in their tiny hamlet as they knew no other way. The men farmed the land, where they grew crops such as wheat and rye for making bread, barley for brewing beer, oats to feed the animals and vegetables such as carrots, parsnips, cabbages and onions, to feed themselves and their families.

They raised pigs for meat, kept sheep which of course could also be eaten, but more importantly, for the wool collected from their fleeces which was spun in into yarn, and then woven into material with which to make their clothing. Cows supplied them with milk, and when the cows became too old and were unable to give anymore milk, they were then slaughtered and their hides supplied all the villagers with the leather for making shoes and belts, and the meat was eaten.

Nothing was ever wasted. Even the cow horns, which were hollow, were made into drinking vessels and their hooves were boiled and made into a glue which had all manner of uses. All Saxon people knew how to reuse anything which could be reused. Today this is known as recycling, but in Saxon times it was simply good sense not to waste anything which could be used again.

Much of the kingdom of the South Saxons was covered in one vast forest which ran from the edge of the sea, northwards, westwards and eastwards for as far as any Saxon man had ever travelled. It was known as The Wildwood and it was full of wolves, wild boar, foxes, deer and many other types of creatures which were scattered throughout the massive woodlands. Some said that even bears still roamed deep within the forest, although no one from Hamm Tun had ever seen one. Therefore, the Wildwood was a place which should only ever have been entered by groups of hunters armed with spears, bows and knives with which to defend themselves from animal attack.

It was also said that there were terrible demons and man-eating dragons living in the forest too, and some nights, as Drefan lay upon his bed made from animal furs laid over a mattress of straw, he would listen to the many strange sounds coming from the mighty Wildwood. Sounds which frightened him and caused him to pull his bedding over his head and hide from the noises made by the creatures of the night.

However, Drefan the Younger was not a coward; far from it. He had killed his first wild boar on a hunting trip into the forest with his father and Eldwyn the Brave only a few weeks earlier. Young Drefan had speared the great boar all by himself, bravely standing his ground as the fierce creature had charged at him, with it's powerful head down and it's large, fearsome tusks slashing wildly at the air.

He had been shaking with fear after the encounter, his small knees knocking together and his hands trembling. But the great boar was dead and the people of Hamm Tun would all eat well that evening, and this made Young Drefan feel very proud of himself. He could also see the pride in his father's eyes as Eldwyn the Brave, dipped his thumb into the blood from the wild boar and made a little circle of red on Young Drefan's forehead.

"There, Drefan son of Drefan. You are now a man as well as a brave hunter!   But the young Drefan was not a man in years, not yet.

He was only eleven years old, quite small for his age and very skinny. He had shoulder length fair hair and deep blue eyes, as did most of the other members of their tribe, although his sister and mother both had darker hair and their eyes were more hazel coloured than blue. He looked very much like his father, yet he, Drefan the Elder, was tall and muscular, with wide shoulders and strong arms and legs. Young Drefan hoped to be just like him when he grew older.

The young boy took to wandering into the woods and exploring the area whenever he had the opportunity, which was not that often, as there was always something which needed to be done around the hamlet. Firewood needed to be collected every day to fuel all the fires which burned continuously in every house. Water was also required on a daily basis for the brewing of a type of weak beer which everyone, including the children drank, and of course for cooking, and that had to be brought in from the stream each and every morning.

In these times, it was safer to brew and drink beer rather than to drink directly from a river or stream, as there was always the risk that the water may have become polluted upstream which could have made them ill, or perhaps even killed them. Something in the brewing process seemed to make the water safe to drink. The beer was very weak and would not have made even the youngest amongst them feel drunk. And anyway, it tasted a lot better than water collected straight from the stream.

There was always help needed with the planting, watering and harvesting of crops throughout the seasons. There were the cows which needed to be milked and the pigs to be fed.

The women were charged with making and mending clothing, brewing the beer and also making a stronger, alcoholic type of beer known as Ale and another drink called Mead which was made from honey. They kept the fires alight, did all the cooking and of course, looked after the younger children as well as a dozen other things.

All of these tasks needed to be completed by the inhabitants of the hamlet every day of the year. There were no such things as holidays or a break for the weekend. These jobs had to be done daily if they were all to survive. They needed to eat, they needed to drink and they needed to keep warm in the winter months, and if they didn't do these things for themselves, then no one else would do it for them, and they would certainly perish.

It was a life of endless hard work, but that was that way people lived in these times. Work hard, or die. There was no other way unless you were fortunate enough to be an Ealdorman or a Theign, and then you had people who would do many of these things for you. But then, he supposed, even an Ealdorman and a Theign had things which they had to do, such as training and then leading men into battle in times of trouble, defending their settlements and those nearby and making and maintaining the laws of the Kingdom.

However, Drefan the Younger decided, it was still a much easier life being a Lord than not being one.

Chapter Two

Once, during the season of summer, when the daylight seemed to last forever and Young Drefan had deliberately finished all of his work extra quickly, he ventured into the Wildwood on his own to explore for a while.

It was all too easy to become lost in those never-ending woods, so he borrowed a trick which he had seen his father use when they had been out hunting one day, and he snapped the twigs on the lower branches of the trees and bushes as he passed by, creating a trail for himself which would lead him back to the safety of the hamlet. At least, he *hoped* it would lead him back.

He walked for what felt like a long time, exactly how long was impossible to tell, as the canopy of trees overhead was so thick that he could not see the sun and he was unable to judge how late it was. It *felt* to him like it was after middle-day, but there was no real way of telling. In these times, there were of course no watches or clocks to tell the time by. Saxon people only had the sun to give them an idea of how the day was passing.

Then ahead, he could see a patch of sunlight shining through the trees into what appeared to be a small clearing in the middle of the dense woodland. As he got closer, he could also see that there was a small, round pond, about the same width across as Eldwyn the Brave's Hall back in Hamm Tun.

The water was completely still and it looked incredibly dark and very deep. Drefan picked up a fallen branch from nearby on the forest floor and prodded the water with it.

He could not feel the bottom of the pool, and as he walked around the edge jabbing with the stick, he realised that the water appeared to be very deep all the way round, as though the edges simply went straight down.

Saxon people, generally speaking, were not able to swim, so he wisely decided to back away from the edge of the water. If he fell in, there would be no one around to help him out again, and he had no intention of drowning in a bottomless pool in the middle of the Wildwood.

He sat on the ground, a pace back from the water's edge and stared into it's depths. Such a strange place for a pool like this, he thought? He could see no stream close by to feed it and it wasn't at the end of a gully which could have directed rainwater towards it? Perhaps there was a natural spring at the bottom of the hole which kept the mysterious pool topped up with water, he mused?

The long walk through the forest had made him hungry, and Drefan remembered the leather pouch containing some nuts and an apple which he had brought with him and he untied it from the twisted hemp belt around his waist. He ate his small meal and lay back on the lush grass which surrounded the pool. He looked up at the almost perfectly round opening in the trees overhead, a slightly larger opening than the pool beneath it. He watched the sky above, his eyes following a small, white cloud as it drifted slowly across in an otherwise clear blue sky.

It was a good day and this was a good place to be, he decided.

He closed his eyes and almost drifted off to sleep, such was the stillness of the Wildwood, for strangely, there was no bird song, no sounds of wild animals nor of the wind blowing through the treetops overhead. It was completely silent and still and peaceful.

He must have actually fallen asleep, because the next thing he was aware of was the noise of something large splashing into the water in the pool beside him, and Drefan suddenly sat bolt upright, drawing his small bony knees up to his chin, his large blue eyes wide and fearful.

There was no sign of anything in the pool, but the water had definitely been disturbed as concentric circles of small waves were radiating out from it's centre, as though something quite large had just jumped, been thrown, or had fallen in.

Drefan scrambled further away from the water's edge and then stood up quickly, looking all around him. There was no sign of anything or anyone that he could see, but then outside of the small clearing around the water hole, the Wildwood quickly became so dark and dense, that a whole *army* of people or forest creatures could have been standing there, and he still would not have been able to spot them.

Strangely, he didn't feel at all scared ; *puzzled*, yes, but certainly not scared. He scratched his head and frowned. **Something** had jumped or fallen into the pool, and something quite large judging by the size of the ripples, which by now had all but stopped. But Drefan could see no trace of anything. Surely if a deer or a wild boar or a wolf had fallen in, there would be **some** sign of it? It would most certainly have struggled its way back up to the surface, and would have made at least *some* sort of effort to escape from the water and clamber back to safety?

As he tried to figure out the mystery of the silent pool, his eyes wandered skywards once more, and he noticed with horror that it looked as though the day was heading towards dusk. He must have been asleep for quite some time!

The Wildwood was definitely not a place to find yourself alone in at night. And *especially* if you were only eleven years old and had no burning torch to light your way nor weapons with which to defend yourself!

Any further thoughts on what had made the ripples in the pool immediately left his head as Drefan dashed back into the forest, his eyes darting quickly from side to side as he urgently looked about him for the tell-tale snapped twigs which would lead him back through the seemingly endless tangle of trees and then home to safety.

His memory tried to ease his fears by telling him that he hadn't *really* been walking through the Wildwood for so very long before he had come across the pool, but as he moved as quickly as he could through the darkening Wildwood, searching desperately for the marks he had left on the trees and bushes, he began to realise that his memory was telling him lies. He **had** been walking for much longer than he remembered, and it was definitely getting darker by the moment.

All about him in the gloom of the forest, he began to imagine that he could hear noises. 'They are just small animals looking for food...squirrels, wood mice and the like...' he told himself. But then the distant howls from a pair of wolves, far off in the great Wildwood reminded Drefan that not *all* the creatures in the forest were either small nor harmless, and he began to panic and broke into a staggering run.

But Drefan, although he was still only young, had the good sense to realise that if he were to lose the trail he had so carefully made during his journey into the forest, he would in all likelihood never leave the Wildwood again. He would *never* find his way home and return back to his father, mother and sister. He would be forever lost in the endless forest and he would continue to struggle his way through the never ending trees and undergrowth until he died of thirst or hunger or worst still, was eaten by hungry wolves, gored to death by a wild boar or captured by one of the many forest demons which the elders had spoken of over the years.

He had no choice; he simply must get out of the Wildwood!

Chapter Three

Drefan the Elder returned to his family's hut after a hard day of labouring at the communal farm and greeted his wife, who was busy cooking the evening meal on the open fire. Drefan nodded to Wilona before he sat, exhausted, and then summoned his daughter.

'Come, Ellette...fetch your poor, hard-working father a refreshing drink on this warm evening!'

Ellette poured him some weak beer from the goat skin hanging from the roof of the hut, and handed the cow horn cup to her father, before she sat down beside him on the reed-covered dirt floor. Drefan the Elder downed the beer in one and held up the horn cup for some more.

As Ellette was about to leap to her feet to refill her father's cup, he laughed heartily and pulled her back, placing his muscular arm around her narrow shoulders and hugging her close to him.

'That can wait, my Ellette! For now, tell me what you and your imp of a brother have been doing with yourselves today? I hope you have both been working hard and behaving for your mother?' He smiled and released the girl, but not before noticing a brief frown appear on her small face.

Drefan adopted his most serious father-face and peered closely at his daughter.

'Ellette....I always know when you are trying to hide things from me. What is it...what has happened?'

The girl squirmed uncomfortably as she realised that she now had both her father *and* mother studying her intently.

'Ellette!' said both parents in unison.

'Well....' she began, uncertainly. 'Drefan and I finished our work earlier than was usual today, and he said that he wanted to go exploring and he told me that I could not go with him.'

Drefan the Elder's frown deepened as she spoke. He knew how foolhardy his son could be sometimes.

'Explore? Explore *where*, exactly?'

Ellette looked nervously from her mother to her father. She didn't like to tell tales, but it was her brother's fault. He should have been back a long time ago, then she wouldn't have had to get him into trouble, because no one would have known anything about it.

'***Ellette!***' barked her mother, angrily.

'He said he was going to explore....in the Wildwood....'

'By Woden! The boy is a fool, and he is surely old enough to know well the dangers of the Wildwood! Even a full-grown man would have to be possessed by madness to venture into the forest alone...and in the darkness too?'

Drefan the Elder leapt to his feet and picked up his spear, which was resting against the wall of the hut and then tucked his seax into his leather belt. He turned to his daughter '**You**...stay here and do not move! Wilona, light some fresh torches and meet me outside after I have roused some of the men!'

Shortly afterwards, Drefan the Elder and a group of six men were gathered in the small central square of the hamlet. Each man was armed with either a spear, bow or seax and each held a flaming torch aloft to light their way ahead along the path which led into the Wildwood.

Even in a well armed group such as theirs, there was still a look of fear in the eyes of some of the men. Saxons were a very superstitious people and the forest was not a place to enter during the hours of darkness. Certainly, no one would ever dream of doing so without very good cause. The Demons of the Wood waited to capture the unwary, and armed or not, every man there knew that spears and knives offered no protection against a malevolent being from the other world.

'Come men, we need to find my son! He is too small to be alone in the Wildwood!' urged Drefan the Elder, and the rest of the men stopped shuffling their feet and looking at the ground and followed him reluctantly as he led the way along the path towards the forest. If it were one of their children lost in the Wildwood, every man present knew that Drefan the Elder would do exactly the same for them.

*****

They had travelled little more than a hundred paces into the forest and yet it already felt as though some huge unknown entity had swallowed them up. It was darker than any night inside the Wildwood, and the feeble light offered by their burning torches only illuminated a small area around the group. Beyond the reach of the guttering flames, everywhere was the blackest of black.

All about them, though completely unseen by the men, they could hear strange and eerie noises. The sounds of creatures of the night, hunting for food, searching by scent alone for their prey in the dense undergrowth and the total darkness.

A wolf suddenly howled far off in the distance and the group paused to make a note of their surroundings and to carefully mark their trail. The very worst thing that could happen now, would be for *them* to become lost in the forest. Although by the light of day, any one of the group would be able to lead them all back safely to the hamlet, but in the overwhelming blackness of the Wildwood at night, however, nobody would feel either confident or brave enough to do so without first carefully marking their route.

They were all set to continue once more, when they heard the snuffling of what could only be a wild boar somewhere in the darkness over to their right. Boar were well known to be fearless creatures who would not think twice about attacking a man, and more especially so if they were defending their young.

So the group halted once again and those with spears raised them in preparation for the attack they feared would soon come.

'Help………help me…..' came a small, frightened voice from the pitch darkness.

'Drefan? Drefan, my son?'

'Father?…….help me!'

Drefan the Elder was gone before anyone else had the chance to follow him. He plunged headlong through the undergrowth and into the darkness, his spear in one hand and his blazing torch held high in the other, sweeping it from side to side as he searched the forest for his only son.

And then he was there! Young Drefan rushed towards the flickering light offered by the torch and threw his skinny arms around his father's waist. Tears were streaming down the boy's grimy face, and snot running from his small nose as he sobbed with relief at seeing his father, and Drefan the Elder hugged him close.

The other men in the group had now joined them, but they stood back a few paces allowing the father and son a brief moment to reunite once more in some sort of privacy.

'Oh, father....I thought I would never get out of the Wildwood! I couldn't find the marks I had made...the way that you had shown me.'

'Enough, Drefan. You are safe and we will talk of this more in the morning. But for now, you must thank every one of these brave men who have come through the dangerous woods to find a foolish young boy.'

Chapter Four

Although Drefan the Young fell into a deep sleep almost as soon as they had returned to the hamlet, he awoke very early the next morning, shortly before cock crow. He was nervous and scared. Nervous about what the other people in the hamlet might think and say about him, and scared as he considered which punishment his father might hand out to him.

He knew that he had been very stupid to go so far into the Wildwood all alone, but he also understood that there was something deep inside him which made him do these things. It was a feeling which he could neither name nor explain, but it made him want to explore and discover new things; travel to places where perhaps others had never heard of or been to. He was scared that this feeling would always be with him, and he feared for where it might lead him to in the future.

Drefan the Young stood timidly before his father Drefan the Elder, Eldwyn the Brave, leader of the hamlet, and the other members of the Council who were all seated upon oak stools placed behind the long feasting table in Eldwyn's Hall house.

The boy stood alone, shaking slightly as he waited to hear his fate. He, Drefan, had potentially risked the lives of several of those men present as well as his own of course, by not only entering the Wildwood alone and unarmed, but almost worse, he had told nobody other than his nine year old sister of where he was heading and why.

'Drefan the Young, we, all the members of the Council here present, have spoken at length about your...what name shall we give this madness? Let us say, your **adventure** of yesterday, when you thought it a good idea to journey alone into the great Wildwood for reasons of your own foolish making. You understand already, I am sure, that you risked not only your own young life in doing that, but you also involved other people who had to come and rescue you from the results of your ridiculous **adventure**.'

Drefan the Young swallowed hard and stared at the ground.

'I am gratified to see that you at least have the wits to look ashamed for what you have done. We...the Council, know that you are not usually an irresponsible or foolish boy. Otherwise the punishment could and most certainly *would* have been much more severe.'

Drefan looked up at the mention of punishment. He swallowed hard once more, and looked imploringly at his father who merely closed his eyes, shook his head briefly, and then turned away. Clearly, the matter was now out of his father's hands. The boy turned his attention to the Elderman once more and he stood erect as he waited for their verdict.

'And so, Drefan the Young....it has been decided that you, and **only** you, will be given the task of clearing up after all the animals in this hamlet, for the period of one moon. This means that you will clean every pig sty, and every cattle fold. If you fail to do this, then be assured that a much harsher punishment will most certainly be delivered upon you.'

Drefan the Young almost sighed aloud with relief. Although mucking out the pigs and the cattle was a truly horrible task, he had in all honestly expected a far worse punishment. And he only had to do it for just one moon? He could do that easily!

'Thank you, Elderman and members of the Council. I know that I truly deserve this punishment and I promise to carry out my tasks without complaint. I apologise sincerely for my stupidity and for risking the lives of the brave men of Hamm Tun.'

Thankfully, Drefan had managed to remember the small speech his mother had rehearsed with him shortly before he had entered the Hall house.

As he turned to leave, Eldwyn the Brave spoke once more; words which stopped Drefan the Young dead in his tracks.

'And of course….there will be no more of these *adventures* into the Wildwood, Drefan the Young. Not until you are a grown man at least. Then you may risk your own life as often as you please!'

*****

Dealing with the animals and removing all of their daily dung piles was pretty disgusting work. Of course, Drefan still had to carry out all his other normal daily tasks as well, such as gathering the firewood and fetching the water from the stream, otherwise it could hardly of been thought of as a punishment. But although it was hard, unpleasant and very smelly work, it felt as nothing compared to him being banned from exploring the Wildwood. That was his *real* punishment. He could contend with mucking out all the animals for a year, *two* years if it meant that he could go exploring again afterwards. But to be forbidden to go into the woods alone until he was a grown man of twelve? That was a cruel punishment indeed.

Chapter Five

It was a full two moons after his punishment had ended, that the young girl Claennis disappeared one sunny afternoon. She was only five years old, and had been playing outside of her family's house with the wooden toys her father had carved for her, when it seems she had simply vanished. Her father had been working on the land at the communal farm and her mother had been busy making and mending some clothes inside the house at the time the girl had disappeared.

Her distraught mother, Nelda, had looked everywhere she could think of, frantically calling her daughter's name aloud before the other women of the hamlet had joined in with the hunt for Claennis. Then the men had been summoned from the fields and a thorough search had been made of every building, outbuilding, cattle fold and ditch in the area.

Nothing, not a single sign of the child was to be found. She must have wandered off into the woods for some unknown reason. It was the only possible place left to for them to look.

And so a search of the forest began, though no one felt very confident that a young child who had wandered off alone into the vast Wildwood, would ever be found alive. But when a tiny fragment of cloth similar to that worn by Claennis was discovered snagged on a thorn bush a few hundred paces inside the forest, the hopes of the people were raised and they continued looking with a new found energy.

Sadly, after searching without a break throughout the rest of that day, there were no further clues to help them find the whereabouts of the missing child, and, as night began to fall, they were forced to return to the hamlet where they were greeted by the hysterical tears of the girl's heartbroken mother.

*****

Several days later, a passing stranger stopped off in the hamlet where he watered his horse and rested for a while. The man, Dreogan, had travelled from another small settlement which was some five days distant from Drefan's hamlet. He had been searching for his young son, also named Dreogan, who, like the missing girl, had simply vanished while playing outside of his father's house just six days earlier.

The similarities were self evident. The man's son was a similar age to the girl at almost six years of age. The disappearance itself was virtually identical. As with the girl, Claennis, the whole of Dreogan's village had thoroughly searched their hamlet before they had then gone into the Wildwood but they had found nothing; no footprints, no marks, no small scraps of cloth. Not a single thing to point to where the boy might have gone. The only difference between the two disappearances was that this man, Dreogan, had borrowed a horse and he had been combing the edges of the Wildwood every day since his son had vanished, but without success.

He did, however, bring news that there had been **another** instance of a child disappearing from outside of their home. In his travels so far, he had heard for certain of only one other. By all accounts it was another boy aged around five years but the Wildwood was so vast and news travelled so very slowly, that he felt there may well be many more stolen children which they had yet to hear tale of.

'And has anyone on your journey had any notions as to what or who could be taking our young ones, Dreogan? Someone must have had **some** sort of an idea as to what is happening to them, surely?' asked Eldwyn the Brave.

'I have heard several theories, Elderman. Some say that it may be one of the many Demons who inhabit the Wildwood. Others think it might be an old crazed Wicce who is said to inhabit the forest and who enjoys the taste of young flesh, while yet more muse that it could be a Knucker Dragon as there are many tales of them inhabiting the woods in these parts in years gone by.' replied Dreogan, shaking his head sadly.

'Well, good Dreogan, we wish you well in your search. If there is anything we can do to help you with your quest, please tell us. We will give you all the help we can.'

'Thank you, Elderman Eldwyn. But other than some food and some ale, there is little else I require. Aside from the blessings of the Gods, that is.'

'Then, may the Gods bless you and your quest, Dreogan.'

*****

When Dreogan the traveller had left to continue with his all but hopeless search, Drefan the Young was left both puzzled and wide-eyed with wonder. His mother was busy brewing ale, but he could not wait for her to finish before he asked, 'What is a Knucker Dragon, mother? I don't think I've ever heard of such a creature?'

Wilona stopped what she was doing, wiped her wet hands down the front of her rough linen dress and looked at her son thoughtfully before replying.

'Hmmm, and you, my lad, were more than lucky not to find out for yourself all about the Knucker the time you went off wandering about in the Wildwood and getting yourself lost and all!'

Drefan frowned. Would she *ever* let him forget about that? He was certain that she felt obliged to mention it to him almost every day.

'But what *is* a Knucker? Is it a real dragon? Do they fly? How big is it? Can it eat people?'

His mother shook her head and smiled. 'One day, my lad, you'll take a breath and stop asking so many foolish questions! Questions, questions, always questions!'

'Please.....?' he pleaded.

Wilona sat down, folded her hands across her lap, sighed deeply and then began to speak.

'I imagine you won't stop your endless chattering until I tell you all that I know about the beast, will you? Well then, a Knucker Dragon is a creature which was spoken of by the Old People. And by all accounts, it is supposed to live in a place called a Knucker Hole. That, so they say, is a bottomless hole which is full of water and the Old People used to tell tales that there are several of them in this very area. Though, I've never seen one myself nor heard of anyone else who has seen one.'

Drefan, his eyes wide with wonder, wiped his mouth with the back of his hand and nodded for his mother to continue.

'There's not much more to be told. The Knucker is said to steal cattle, sheep and sometimes people to feed itself, but that is only supposed to happen if a person is foolish enough to live right near a Knucker Hole. Anyone who set up house near one of those would soon be moving on...if they lived long enough to escape from the Dragon, of course!'

Drefan sat open mouthed, his large blue eyes now even wider with astonishment.

'Right, I have work to be getting on with, Drefan, even if you don't, so you had better find yourself something to do, or else I'll find something for you!' His mother stood up and went back to her brewing.

'Just one last question, Mother....please?'

'One question...and that's it, Drefan the Young. Or you'll not live long enough to become Drefan the Old! What is it?'

'How *large* do you think a Knucker Dragon grows and how big would a Knucker Hole be?'

'That's *two* questions, you young imp! As I told you, no one of my acquaintance has ever seen a Knucker Dragon, so I have no idea and cannot tell you how big they grow. But, if it is indeed true that they can eat a full grown cow, I'm imagining that they are fairly large. As for a Knucker Hole...well, I would take a guess and say that they are about the size of.....oooh, about the size of Eldwyn's Hall as an example, and the Old People used to say that these holes are perfectly round and completely bottomless. Now, you get yourself out of here and find someone else to pester before I make *you* completely bottomless, my lad!'

Chapter Six

That night Drefan could not sleep. His mind was full of visions of what he imagined a Knucker Dragon might look like. He was almost certain that the strange, round pool he had discovered way out in the Wildwood **must** have been a Knucker Hole; the place where the Old People supposed the Knucker Dragon dwelt. Then he thought about that strange splash in the pool which had woken him up so suddenly. But wouldn't a Knucker Dragon be huge and wouldn't it have made a **much** bigger splash than the one he had heard?

Drefan must have finally fallen into a troubled sleep, because the next thing he knew, it was cock crow and his mother was up and busy preparing food so that they could break their fast before the day's work commenced.

Saxon people usually built their houses with the entrance facing towards the South so that they could take advantage of as much natural daylight as possible, and Drefan could already feel the gentle heat from the early morning sun upon his back as he sat by the doorway, eating his meal and sipping his weak beer.

'Come, young Trouble. We have much work to get done this fine morning so hurry up and break your fast and let us get on with it.' said his father just as Drefan was finishing his rye bread and washing the last piece down with his weak beer. Wiping his mouth with the back of his hand, Drefan handed his wooden bowl and cow horn beaker back to his mother and jumped to his feet.

'I'm ready, father.' and the two men of the house set off for their day's labours, leaving the two women behind to complete their own chores.

*****

It was around middle-morning, when Baldlice, one of Eldwyn's three sons, came rushing into the field where most of the men of the hamlet were busy working. He had obviously been running in the heat of the day, as he was sweating heavily, red faced and panting hard. He stood bent over for a while resting, as he waited for his breath to return, and then he shouted.

'It's little Aedre...' he gasped, 'Aedre has disappeared!'

Everyone stopped what they were doing, put down whatever tools they had been using and walked across to Baldlice. The boy was well known for his often stupid jokes, and the men were tempted to ignore him at first. But the look on his face and the way that he stood convinced them that perhaps this time he was actually telling the truth.

'My father has sent me to gather all the men of the hamlet! I speak the truth, I swear. Aedre has been taken, just as Claennis was taken.' The look on the boy's face was enough for the men to believe what he was saying, and they followed him back to Hamm Tun where Eldwyn was waiting, along with Aedre's distraught mother and the rest of the women who were doing their best to comfort her.

Once again, all the men of the hamlet ventured into the Wildwood, only this time many of the women joined them as well, as they did not wish to be left back in Hamm Tun when they could be more useful helping in the search for the missing girl. Eldwyn's wife Mildred and their daughter Maida stayed behind to console Sibley, Aedre's mother as she was far too upset to join the others and would probably have hindered rather than helped in the search for the missing girl.

Just as before, it was almost dark before the search parties returned, and as before, they were empty handed. There had been absolutely no trace of Aedre. Not so much as a footprint or the smallest scrap of material had been found, and this time they had ventured even further into the Wildwood than ever before, splitting up into four separate groups so that the greatest area of woodland could be searched.

*****

As was becoming his habit of recent nights, Drefan found it almost impossible to get off to sleep. He was *convinced* that the Knucker Dragon had something to do with all these disappearances, and he was *certain* that he had discovered the Knucker Hole out there, deep in the Wildwood.

But who would believe him, a mere boy? And a boy called 'Trouble' at that? He would either end up becoming the laughing stock of Hamm Tun, or he would get punished for talking about a dragon at a time when most of the adults were far too busy worrying about their own children disappearing, to listen to his tales of Knucker Dragons living in a bottomless pool, way out in the forest.

Just before he finally went to sleep, he had made up his mind. He would go back into the Wildwood once again to try to find the girl and he would gladly suffer any punishment dealt out to him if he failed. But either way, *someone* had to take a look at that Knucker Hole, and he knew that it would be up to him and him alone.

He realised that there would be serious consequences for him when he returned, so he made a point of telling his sister, Ellette, where he was going and why. He begged her not to tell their mother and father of his plan until he had been gone for at least a half a day, as he guessed that his father would immediately start searching for him as soon as he discovered where he had gone.

Chapter Seven

This time, Drefan had been much better prepared for his journey through the Wildwood. He had borrowed his father's best seax to help him mark out a much clearer trail. He would do this by cutting several branches at a time along the way, instead of just snapping the odd one here and there as he had done previously. And, as he looked back to check on his work, he could see that *this* track was much easier to follow than the other one had been.

He had also left home a lot earlier than he had the previous time. Drefan hadn't carried out any of his daily chores that morning other than fetching the water, and he had left Hamm Tun way before cock crow, so he knew that this would give him a lot more daylight time than before. He knew that he had travelled many furlongs, quite how many, he had no idea, but his legs told him that he had certainly come a long way.

Drefan tried as best he could to follow the markings he had made on his earlier journey into the great Wildwood, but he soon understood why he hadn't been able to find them in the darkening forest the last time. They were far too small and very easy to miss. This time, however, Drefan made certain that they would be much easier to spot.

Then finally, he could see the small circular clearing off to the left of where he stood, and he made his way through the thick woodland and undergrowth towards it. Once again, he looked behind him to make certain that his trail markers were easy to see. He did not want to get lost or spend a single heartbeat longer than he needed to in the Wildwood after darkness fell.

*****

The pool was exactly as he remembered it. About a rod across and almost perfectly round, full of very dark-looking, completely still water.

There were no marks anywhere around the edges of the pool. No, it wasn't *just* a pool; it was the Knucker Hole for certain, he just knew it was. However, there were no signs that the Knucker had visited the Hole recently, but then again what signs should he be looking for? No one he knew had ever seen a Knucker, so neither he nor anyone else of his acquaintance could describe how big or small the dragon was likely to be, what it might look like or how fierce it might become.

Strangely, Drefan thought, there were no animal tracks of any kind around the pool? The Wildwood covered a vast area and he knew for certain that it was full of many types and sizes of creatures, yet it would seem that not a single one of them had come to the pool to take a drink? And as far as Drefan could see, there were no other water sources anywhere near the Knucker Hole. Could the creatures of the Wildwood perhaps sense that a Knucker Dragon lived in the Hole?

The more he thought about that, the more certain he became that he had *indeed* found the home of the Knucker. If all the other animals living within the woods were too scared to come to it and drink, including the fierce wolves and the wild boar, then there *must* be something far larger and much more terrifying hereabouts to frighten them all away!

Drefan's eyes widened as these thoughts came into his head. If a *wolf* was scared of a Knucker, then what did he, a skinny, eleven year old boy think he would do if the Knucker appeared?

He slowly backed away from the edge of the Knucker Hole, looking nervously all about him as he returned into the cover of the thick undergrowth. He took a deep breath, and sat down on the trunk of a fallen tree to think about what he should do next. It would be no use at all to return to Hamm Tun and tell his father and the men of the Council about this Knucker Hole. Not unless he could find some sort of proof to show them. Otherwise they would just laugh at his craziness and punish him worse than they had the last time.

Finally, he decided that he would explore the Wildwood surrounding the Knucker Hole and see if he could find something, *anything* that he could take back to the hamlet and show to the others.

Drefan walked slowly and carefully through the dense woodland, trying to be as quiet as he could, but it was almost impossible not to make a sound as the forest floor was littered with dried leaves and twigs which snapped as he stepped upon them.

He carefully scanned the ground around him as he walked, looking for anything which might be a sign that a Knucker Dragon had been this way, though it was very difficult as he had no idea of what he was looking for exactly.

Before he realised it, Drefan had done a complete circle of the Knucker Hole and he was now back where he had started once more. And he had found precisely **nothing**!

So, he took five long strides to his right and did the same thing all over again. Still nothing. Another five strides to his right. He was now quite some distance from the Knucker Hole, three rods at least, so this new search circle would be much wider and take a lot longer to travel around, but he knew that he had to keep trying.

He was approximately half way around this new circle, when he thought he heard a sound coming from somewhere directly ahead of him, but it was quite some way off in the distance. He stood completely still and listened very carefully.

There was nothing for a short while, and then he heard it again. It sounded like a sort of strange wailing noise. Not the kind of sound which would be made by any animal he thought, at least, not any animal that **he** knew of?

He began to make his way slowly towards the sound, when another, similar noise joined the first one coming from the same area, and as he got a little closer, he finally realised what those sounds were.

It was children crying! And at least two of them he judged.

He hurried towards the noise as quickly as the dense undergrowth and the hidden tree roots would allow and the closer he got, the louder the crying became, until he was standing beneath a mighty old oak tree which towered high above him, it's top way higher than all the other trees which surrounded it.

Now he could clearly hear the children crying, and it sounded to Drefan as though there were *more* than two of them!

'Hello....you, up in the tree! Who are you?' he yelled. At first, they did not hear him calling as they were making too much noise with their crying and wailing, so Drefan tried once more.

'You...in the tree! Who are you?' he yelled at the top of his lungs, cupping his hands about his mouth to make his voice sound louder.

And then finally; **'Help us! Please, help us!'** came a reply, followed by; **'Please...get us down from here...we are trapped!'** There was a babble of young children's voices, so definitely more than two of them up there, but they were all talking at once and he could hardly understand what they were saying to him.

'*Stop!*' he yelled at the top of his voice. 'Just *one* of you speak, or I cannot help you!' There was a moment of panic when the children thought he might not rescue them, but after a few moments, Drefan heard, 'I am Claennis..I shall speak for us all.'

Drefan could hardly believe his own ears.'*Claennis*? Is it really *you*? It's me...Drefan, come to find you!'

'*Drefan?* Can it be you?'

'Aye, it's me, Claennis. Tell me, how many are you?'

'There are four of us all together....Aedre is here...she was brought only yesterday. Then there are two boys. They are not from our hamlet. They are called Dreogan and Leof....both are from different villages. Can you rescue us, Drefan?'

'I'll do my best. I might have to go back and get help from the hamlet though…'

'***NO! It might come back before then!***' screamed Claennis and the other children began sobbing wildly once again.

Drefan stepped away from the huge oak tree and looked up to the first few branches high above him. He was a good climber, but this tree was very tall. And climbing up would be one thing, however bringing four youngsters back down with him would be almost impossible? There were no branches lower down the trunk for him to begin his climb, and the girth of the giant oak was far too wide for him to hug the tree and climb it that way.

He stepped further back from the oak and looked all around him.

There were a few smaller trees surrounding the mighty oak, and one of them, a beech tree, had lower branches which would be far easier for him to scramble up. Near the top of the beech tree, it appeared as though its branches overlapped with the lower branches of the oak tree, and it might be possible for him to climb across from one tree to the other. Then, once he was in the oak tree, it should be straightforward enough for him to climb up and reach the children.

But, he still had to somehow get them all back down to the ground again? And then he remembered his father's seax, tucked into his belt.

'Wait for a just a while longer!' he called up, 'I have to make a rope of some kind.'

'Please..*hurry*! It might come back!'

'I'll be as quick as I can!' replied, Drefan.

Chapter Eight

It didn't take him very long to find enough creepers and vines in the Wildwood to fashion a length of basic rope. It would surely not have tethered an angry wild boar for very long, but it would have to do for his purposes.

He coiled the rope about his narrow shoulders and began climbing the beech tree as quickly as he could. Within a short time he had reached the top and very carefully, he stretched out across to the branches of the oak tree, making sure not to look down as it was a long drop back to the forest floor.

Slowly, he clambered from the beech tree and made his way across to the trunk of the old oak and from there, he was able to climb up toward the top.

As he glanced up, he saw high above him something which resembled a huge bird's nest, only this was made from strong, thick branches and it was packed with leaves and pieces of turf, rather than the usual twigs and moss of a normal nest.

As he climbed closer, he could see that the nest was at least the width of a grown man standing upright and it was deep and very strongly made. It was shaped like a huge bowl and it was nestled in the fork of three massive branches near the very top of the tree.

Finally, he reached the 'nest' and he cautiously clambered inside to be greeted by the four terrified youngsters, who were all sobbing wildly as they hugged their rescuer.

When Drefan regained his breath, he said,

'Stop your blubbering...all of you! I have to get you out of here and back down to safety and we can't do that if you're all snivelling!' His words had the desired effect and one by one, the children fell silent.

'Good! Now, I can't carry you down, so you are going to have to climb. Just take your time, climb slowly and carefully and all will be well. When we get closer to the bottom, I will lower you down to the ground with this rope. Is everyone ready?'

The four young children nodded.

'Right then...follow me and do exactly as I do.'

The hardest part was actually leaving the 'nest', as they had to climb over the edge and then feel for the branches beneath with their feet, but they all got the hang of it soon enough and surprisingly quickly, they had managed to clamber down the giant oak tree and were perched precariously on the thick lower branches, waiting for Drefan to tie the rope around their waist before he lowered each of them down to the ground. The ground which was still at least the height of three tall men below them.

When the last child was safely on the forest floor, Drefan wrapped one end of the rope about the branch, tied it securely and then lowered himself, hand over hand down to join them.

'Right....now we must make our way back to Hamm Tun as quickly and as quietly as we can, and then we will tell the men of the Council everything that has happened here.'

'But the **creature**! It will capture us and eat everyone!' wailed Aedre, her eyes wide with terror.

'It cannot eat you if you are not here, now can it? So get moving...*go!*'

*****

Drefan was quickly able to pick up his trail this time, and was very pleased that he had made the effort to make the marks so much clearer. The four children followed along in a line behind him, walking in a nervous silence, and only speaking if they stumbled on a hidden tree root or snagged themselves on a bramble.

It was difficult as always in the Wildwood to tell the time of the day, but it seemed to Drefan that there was still plenty of daylight left, and they would hopefully all be back in Hamm Tun well before darkness fell.

Only once did one of the boys ask that they might stop for a while to rest, but Drefan quickly reminded him of the nest up in the oak tree, and of the Knucker Dragon who had placed him there and the boy soon changed his mind and carried on with a renewed energy.

Some time later, Drefan heard the sound of heavy footsteps in the distance, and he beckoned the others to get down and keep still. If they remained quiet and unmoving, he was certain that nothing would be able to find them as they hid in the thick undergrowth.

Then he heard raised voices; someone was yelling his name, and he rushed forwards towards the sound, the others following slowly behind him.

As Drefan emerged suddenly from behind a dense thicket, he was almost stabbed by a spear wielded by Eldwyn.

'Curse you, boy! I could have skewered you like a hog then!'

Drefan the Elder was beside the Elderman, and although Drefan the Young could tell that he was mightily relieved to see his son once again, he could also sense that his father was furious with him.

'Damn you, Drefan! Trouble by name and trouble by nature! How many more times will you have us out to look for you in the Wildwood, boy?'

It was then that the ragged bunch of young children appeared as they struggled their way through the undergrowth towards the search party, and every man present stood with their eyes wide and their mouth open in astonishment.

'I'm sorry, Father.....but I thought that I might find them if I looked hard enough...'

Chapter Nine

There was a great feast held in Hamm Tun that night, in honour of Drefan the Young and the safe return of the missing children. Drefan was, and rightly so, hailed as a hero for finding them and for bringing them back to safety.

The following morning, riders were sent out to return the two boys back to their own settlements, and when they returned several days later, they brought with them much praise and many gifts for Drefan, which had been donated by the grateful parents of Dreogan and Leof.

But the question of exactly how the children had been taken and by what, was still a matter for great discussion.

Drefan the Young had tried to convince the people of his hamlet that it was all the work of a Knucker Dragon, and the children who had been taken also confirmed that it was definitely a

Dragon which had snatched them as they had played, and had then flown them and placed them into the nest, high up in the mighty oak in the deep Wildwood.

However, no one could agree over **why** a Knucker should behave in such an odd way? All of the legends which had been passed down by word of mouth from the Old People had said, that if a Knucker Dragon was hungry, it would take sheep or cattle, and very rarely, men, women or young children. But it would always **eat** its prey. It surely would not have left them in a nest high up in an oak tree before going out once more to hunt and capture yet more food?

None of it made any sense. Maybe the children had simply imagined the Knucker Dragon? Perhaps Drefan had told them about the Knucker and they had just agreed with him in their state of terror and confusion? But then, how in the name of Woden and all the Gods had they all ended up in the great oak tree, out there in the depths of the Wildwood?

Drefan told the Council that the only way he could think of convincing them that the Knucker Dragon was real, was for him to take them back into the Wildwood so that they could see for themselves. That way they could be certain, one way or another, and they could then decide what they should do next.

One thing, however, **was** decided that day; no child was ever to be allowed to play outside on its own until the matter of the Knucker Dragon was settled. They had been very fortunate, and had it not been for the bravery of Drefan the Young, who knows what might have happened to those four young children.

*****

Drefan had another of his strange dreams that night. This one, was the strangest of them all, by far.

He dreamt that he was underwater and at the bottom of a deep, dark, cold pool. He could feel the chill of the water pressing all about him, and it was completely black with no light coming from anywhere. He was totally alone and he felt incredibly sad. He was certain that the terrible sensation of loneliness was the reason for his sadness.

Bizarrely, he also knew that he was now a female. He had no idea *how* he knew this fact, but he just did.

Then quite suddenly, he was rising up through the dark, cold water, moving faster and faster until he burst out from the inky blackness of the pool and found himself/herself flying, up and up and up into the night sky, high above the great Wildwood which spread out below in every direction, the trees clearly lit up by the light from a full moon.

And as he/she flew, they began to understand the reason for their terrible sadness and loneliness, for suddenly, there was another of their kind flying alongside, a big male Knucker Dragon who swooped and twisted and turned playfully, beside the Drefan Dragon, and the

Drefan Dragon knew at that moment, that they were mates, male and female partners and she could sense that they had known one another for many, many years.

But then in an instant, the big male was no longer there. Drefan Dragon could see humans...***men-kind***, and they had killed her mate. Those men-kind had fired a huge arrow up into the sky and it had struck the large male in his chest, and brought him crashing down into the forest far below. And then, while she circled in the sky far above, she watched as the humans cut off her beloved's head and placed it upon a spike. Then, the evil men-kind chopped him up into small pieces and they burnt those pieces upon a huge fire. They removed his teeth and pulled out all of his claws and they decorated their necklaces with them, and they danced and they laughed and they cheered as they celebrated his death. His ***murder***!

However, all of this, Drefan Dragon sensed, had happened a long, long time ago; many years before. In a time long before the Saxon peoples had come to live in this land. Way back in the time when people who were called themselves Romans had inhabited the country and they had been terrified of the Knucker Dragons and had tried to slaughter every one they could find. Even though no Knucker had ever harmed a man-kind and even though they only took the occasional sheep or young calf when they could not find enough food in the vast Wildwood.

This, it seemed, had been enough to make these Roman humans hate the Knucker and want to destroy them all.

Drefan could feel the terrible pain of the female Knucker. He could feel the loss of her mate and her horrible loneliness and her dreadful, overwhelming sadness. He could also sense her fear; fear that the Romans would do the same to her as they had done to her mate.

And so she had fled, deep into the Wildwood to a place where no human creature had ever set foot. Far away from the man-kind and their towns and villages, far away from the Romans with their terrible arrows which could bring down a Knucker in mid-flight.

She had discovered the pool, the Knucker Hole as it would become known, and she sank down into its depths, down into the safety of the cold, dark, deep water where she remained for so many moons, that no man could count them. Not that she could see the moon of course, as she hid down there in the dark water of the Knucker Hole.

And she slept.

Down in the depths of the Knucker Hole she had remained for hundreds of human years, before one day awakening once more, and finding herself all alone in the darkness.

She had been scared, still, even after all those long years. And still she felt lonely; very, very lonely.

But, Knucker Dragons are amazing and incredibly ancient creatures, and within her body she could feel a strange sensation. She instinctively understood, that there was a new life growing deep inside her body. She knew that she was carrying a young Knucker Dragon, one which had been created by herself and her murdered mate shortly before he had been murdered, and, as she had slept through those long, dark years at the bottom of the Knucker Hole, a baby Knucker had been growing slowly, as it took many, many years for a new Knucker life to come into the world.

And so instinctively the female Knucker had begun to carefully build herself a nest, high up in the tallest and strongest tree she could find. Far away from the animals of the forest and more importantly, as far away from the human kind as was possible. The nest took her a long time to build but when it was finished, it was a fine, strong one which could easily hold her and the newborn Knucker in complete safety when it finally came into the world.

And then, for no apparent reason, she had begun to feel very ill. She had not been able to eat for many days, and the terrible pains deep inside her had left her feeling too weak to leave the nest and go out to hunt. She lay there, unable to sleep but also unable to move and the long days had passed by very slowly.

Then at last, the time had come and she gave birth to her young Knucker Dragon. The product of herself and her beloved mate, created so many years before in a time when they had known only happiness and joy.

But the baby Knucker did not move.

She prodded it gently with her snout, and then she shook it firmly, trying to bring life into the tiny creature, but it lay there in the large nest still and unmoving.

Her baby, like her mate, was dead. Stillborn, after growing inside her for so many years.

*****

The female Knucker had been driven almost insane with grief. Her brain and her body told her that she was a mother, yet there was nothing for her **to** mother. There **was** nothing left for her to love and to nurture. It was just her and her alone, and that was the way it would now always be. Only her, as there were no longer any other Knucker Dragons left in the land.

The Roman humans had killed them all, because of their fear and their hatred for a creature which they simply did not understand. Even though she had slept for hundreds of human years, she somehow knew that she was the last of her kind. There were no others, of that she was certain.

And that was when she had stolen the first child. A small human boy, who had been playing quietly just outside of his house near the Wildwood. It had been all so easy for her to swoop down on silent wings and snatch the young boy up, holding him very gently in her claws and then fly off before anyone could notice, returning to her nest deep in the Wildwood, close to the Knucker Hole.

But the child had made a strange and pitiful noise almost from the moment she had picked it up until she had placed it in the nest. A high-pitched wailing sound which had upset her greatly. She had tried feeding the boy with the small animals she had caught in the Wildwood, but it didn't seem to make any difference. The boy simply ignored the food and he continued to wail incessantly.

So she took another small child, in exactly the same way as the first. This time, she selected a female, only this one seemed to wail even louder and for longer than the first! However, the two of them at least communicated with one another sometimes as they huddled together in the Knucker nest, and that stopped them from making those terrible noises.

But the nest had still looked so large and so empty, and the creatures she had brought back were so small and so feeble that the Knucker felt she needed to find more of them to fill it up. And so the other two children were gathered up and brought back, which made the nest look full, and that made the Knucker feel happy.

She would bring food to the children every third day, and the rest of her time she would spend at the bottom of her Knucker Hole, far away from the world of men-kind, safe down there in the darkness. But she still felt so incredibly lonely. No human child could ever replace the mate she had lost, nor her own stillborn infant.

Chapter Ten

When Drefan awoke at cock-crow the next morning, he knew exactly what the villagers needed to do.

He asked to meet Eldwyn the Brave and the other members of the Council, and he told them of the dream he had the night before. He explained what had happened to the Knucker Dragon and he told them of her terrible grief and loss. Normally, the elders would have laughed at a young boy talking in such a way, but since Drefan had found and rescued the children, returning them safely and at great risk to himself, they were prepared to at least listen to what he had to say.

'And so, please.... we must not slay the Knucker. She has surely suffered enough already, and it would simply be cruel to punish her for what she has done?'

There was a mumbling of voices as the Eldwyn and the other members of the council discussed what they had just heard.

'Dreams? Female Knucker Dragons? Nests in an oak tree? The Romans??'

While the Councillors argued amongst themselves, Drefan sat cross-legged on the floor of the Hall and waited patiently. Some of the voices were raised, and others spoke calmly, while just occasionally one of the council members would glance across at Drefan and frown, before returning to the discussion.

'But how do we know that any of this nonsense is true? He is but an eleven year old boy, for Woden's sake!'

Finally, Eldwyn raised his hands and the others fell silent.

'Young Drefan here found the pool in the Wildwood all by himself several moons ago. And then, he tells us, he had a dream that the pool was a Knucker Hole. Finally, when little Aedre was taken, Drefan dreamt that he should go into the Wildwood and find the Knucker Hole once more, as he was sure that the answer to the disappearances lay close to that spot?'

The others all nodded in agreement with the facts so far.

'So doesn't it stand to reason, therefore, that if Drefan was brave enough to risk his own life in the Wildwood because of *those* dreams, then why could this *latest* dream not be an omen, also? If he was right on those previous occasions, then why should it not be so this time?'

The elders looked at one another, and nodded their heads once more. Eldwyn, as usual, had made things clear for them. They all had to agree that his argument made very good sense.

And so, it was decided that the Knucker Dragon would not be slain. But what **would** happen to her? They could not just leave her to continue snatching young children whenever she felt like it, or perhaps something even worse in the future.

Because the people of Hamm Tun had agreed that she should not be harmed, it did not necessarily follow that people in other hamlets and larger villages would feel the same way about the creature and be so lenient with it?

It was a genuine problem, and one which the Councillors were giving serious thoughts to. But Drefan already had an idea.

'I would like you to give me permission to go back to the Knucker Hole, please?' he asked.

The Councillors stopped their discussion and looked towards Drefan, their faces very puzzled. Eldwyn said,'If you really think it will help? I will arrange for you to be escorted there with a band of armed men, young Drefan.'

Drefan smiled and shook his head.

'No...please, sir...I would like to go alone. I feel it is the only way to end this?' Drefan the Elder drew a breath ready to argue with his son, but Eldwyn placed his hand on the man's arm.

'Be calm, Drefan. Your son is wise way beyond his years, and no harm has come to him during his previous travels into the Wildwood, after all?'

Drefan the Elder considered this, before saying, 'He will be wiser still if he takes my seax with him...just in case?'

The young Drefan smiled, and glanced at the knife which his father held out for him. He took it and tucked the seax into his hempen belt.

'Thank you, father, but I hope that I shall not be needing a weapon.'

*****

The next morning, at the break of dawn, Drefan the Young headed out from his home into the Wildwood yet again, only this time, he was escorted part of the way by his father and Eldwyn the Brave.

'Are you sure that this is the only way, Drefan?' asked the Elderman.

Drefan smiled,. 'Nothing is for certain, sir, but I can at least try this way first.'

His father hugged him close and then he was gone, swallowed up by the great Wildwood as he headed towards the Knucker Hole and whatever lay ahead.

Chapter Eleven

Even though this was the third time that Drefan had travelled to the clearing in the forest, he was still very careful to make sure that he followed the marks which he had made previously. A person could pass through these woods a hundred times and yet still not remember the way and become lost forever in the Wildwood.

Fortunately, the marks he had so carefully made the last time, still looked fresh enough to follow with ease, and this made his journey much easier and a lot quicker than the other times. His mind was so occupied with his thoughts, that before he realised it he could see the clearing through the trees less than a rod away.

When he grew closer, he slowed his pace and walked as quietly as he could.

As usual, there was no sign of life at the Knucker Hole. There were no footprints around the edge of the pool, and this to Drefan's mind , confirmed that the Knucker Dragon was still down there, slumbering in its depths.

In his dream, the Knucker had emerged every three days to feed the children in the nest, and by his calculations, today would be the third day. Drefan had left Hamm Tun very early and had made good time through the Wildwood, so he estimated that it was not even mid-morning yet.

He sat cross-legged right at the edge of the Knucker Hole and took a handful of nuts from the pouch at his belt. As he sat munching his snack, he noticed for the first time since he had been coming to that place, a steady stream of bubbles rising up from the depths of the pool. The bubbles were small at first, but they gradually grew larger and larger when quite suddenly, the waters parted and Drefan was looking directly into the face of a Knucker Dragon!

Drefan fell backwards in surprise and the Knucker did exactly the same, toppling backwards into the dark pool from where it had just emerged.

Quickly, Drefan gathered his wits and scrambled to his feet, stepping back a couple of paces from the edge of the pool, just as the Knucker broke the surface once more and made it's way across to the other side of the Knucker Hole where she slowly slithered out of the water and stood studying the boy who stood opposite her.

It was almost comical the way that the two looked so cautiously at one another, each of them full of distrust for the other.

The Knucker was much smaller than Drefan had imagined it to be. Her body was about the length and width of a cow, and she had a long, scaly tail of around the same length as her body. She was also much shorter than he had imagined she would be; around the height of one of the wild forest ponies. She had a broad head on a long neck, and again, her head was of a similar size to a cow or a pony, but much wider and she had two very long pointed ears.

There were also, as you would expect for a dragon, a set of very sharp and very pointed teeth, some of which protruded from her upper jaw and measured as long as a man's thumb. She had very large, bright yellow eyes, like those of a cat.

Her legs, although not very long, we're powerfully built, and her feet were splayed and had large toes which could almost have acted like flippers in the water, and each toe also had a long and dangerous looking sharp claw which appeared to be retractable, again, very similar to a cat's claws.

The Knucker was a greeny-grey colour and covered in tough-looking scales that were larger on it's back and along its flanks, but they became much smaller on its underside, and they glinted slightly in the sunlight which filtered into the clearing.

But *the* most amazing thing about her, was the pair of huge, leathery wings which were folded neatly along the entire length of her back! On the inside, they were bright red in colour with green boney spines. They looked very similar to a bat's wings, although of course many times bigger. The outside of her wings were the same colour as her body, so that the incredible red colour could only be seen once she spread them wide.

Drefan was the first one to move.
He rummaged in the willow basket he had strung across one shoulder and removed a large fish, which he had asked Bowden the fisherman to catch for him the day before. Drefan held the fish out in front of him and slowly, and carefully he made his way around the pool towards the Knucker Dragon.

He had absolutely no idea whether Knucker Dragons liked or ate fish, but he somehow felt that as a water dragon, they probably did.

The Knucker sniffed the air, and she blinked those huge yellow eyes which showed recognition. She took a small step towards Drefan, while Drefan continued to move very slowly and cautiously towards her. Finally, they were just over an arm's length apart, and the

Knucker moved her large head forwards, gently taking the fish from Drefan's hand in the way that a hound might take a piece of meat from it's master.

It was quite a large fish but to the Knucker, it was a very small snack. Two bites and the fish was gone and she stood there looking at Drefan, with an unfathomable expression on her strange-looking face. Drefan brought out the second fish from the basket, and held it out in front of the Knucker.

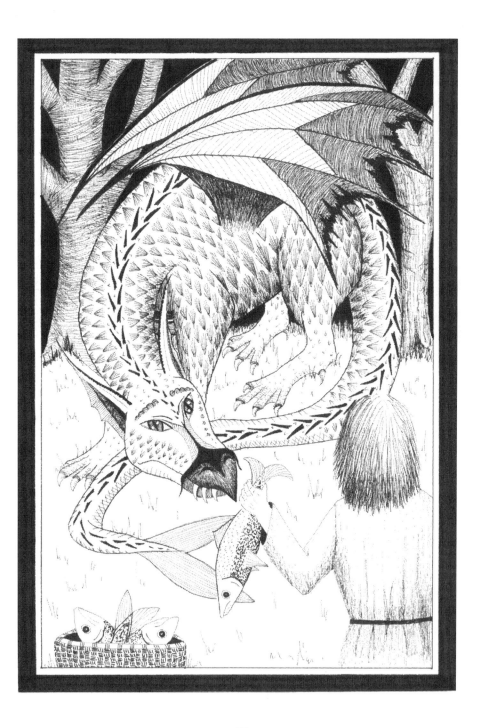

95

Once again, she took it very gently from Drefan's outstretched hand and gobbled it up in two bites. After she had devoured the third and last of the fish he had brought with him, Drefan held out his hands in front of him, palms uppermost, in an attempt to show the Knucker that there was no more food. She watched him carefully for a moment with her large yellow eyes and then leant across and sniffed his hands, before retreating backwards slightly.

This was it, thought Drefan. It would be now or never.

Very slowly, he stepped forward once again, until he was within touching distance of the Knucker. The Knucker stayed where she was, an unmistakable puzzled expression in her eyes as she watched to see what this human was going to do next.

Drefan moved his hand forward and placed it on the side of the Knucker Dragon's head. He waited for a moment, and when nothing had happened, he began to gently stroke her head, slowly moving his hand down and then stroking her under her chin.

Suddenly, and quite unexpectedly, the Knucker Dragon let out a long, shuddering sigh before she squatted down on her hind legs as Drefan continued to gently caress the creature. They stayed this way for a long time, with Drefan finally kneeling down beside the Knucker when she closed her large yellow cat-like eyes and lay down completely, allowing the human to continue to soothe her .

*****

Meanwhile, back under the cover of the Wildwood, Eldwyn, Drefan the Elder and several other men from the village, looked on in amazement at the sight before them. Firstly, none of them had ever seen a Knucker Dragon before, and secondly, no one could believe that a small boy could actually befriend such a fearsome-looking beast, and was in fact petting the creature as though it were nothing more terrifying than a hound or a cat!

They had secretly followed Drefan through the Wildwood, mostly because they feared for his safety, but partly because if there **was** a Dragon living in there, they needed to see it for themselves.

The heavily armed men continued to watch the amazing spectacle for a while longer, before they headed back to the hamlet. There was no need to let Drefan know what they had witnessed and they would keep the secret strictly amongst those present.

Chapter Twelve

And so, from that day onwards, the Knucker Dragon of the Wildwood near Hamm-tun, was no longer thought of as a threat by the people who lived nearby.

Every third day, Drefan would make the long trip through the Wildwood back to the Knucker Hole with his basket full of fish, and he would feed the Knucker before they spent time in one another's company for a while. Sometimes, Drefan would take the two girls, Claennis and Aedre along with him and they would all take it in turns to feed the Knucker and sit with her until it was time for them to leave.

The Knucker never took another a child and she never felt lonely again. To this day, there are still Knucker Holes to be seen in West Sussex and there have been various tales over the years of Knucker Dragons stealing cattle and children, before they were either slain by a brave knight or killed after eating a poisoned pie.

But this is the only *true* story……

Saxon names and words used in this story.

NAME/WORD:	MODERN MEANING:
Drefan...Dre-fan......................	Trouble
Wilona...Will-oaner...................	Hoped For
Ellette...Ell-et...........................	Little Elf
Eldwyn...Eld-win......................	Wise Advisor
Claennis...Clay-nis...................	Purity
Baldlice...Bald-lice...................	Bold
Aedre...Air-dree......................	Stream
Dreogan...Dree-o-gan..............	Suffer
Mildred...Mil-dred....................	Gentle advisor
Maida...Made-a.......................	Maiden
Sibley...Sib-lee.......................	Friendly

Elderman..............not to be confused with an Ealdorman. Elderman is usually the oldest man in the settlement, (literally elder man) and therefore thought to be the wisest. Leader of the Council.

Ealdorman...Eel-dor-man....... A high ranking official who was in charge of one or more Shires. A combination of an Administrator, Military Commander and a Judge. Later, the name would be altered to Earl.

Theign...Thane...............A person ranked between an Ealdorman and an ordinary Freeman. A Lord who held land given by the King for services rendered.

Seax...See-ax.............a long knife or dagger used in Saxon times.

Hamm-Tun.....The farm or hamlet near a river meadow

(Later this would become Hampton and later still, Littlehampton to differentiate it from the much larger Southampton, in Hampshire)

Englaland...original meaning - the Land of the Angles

Rod........equivalent of 15 Saxon feet (1 Saxon foot is 13.2 modern inches)

Furlong.........................equal to 10 Rods

Wind eyes....which is where we get our word **windows** from. They were small, usually triangular shaped holes cut into the wooden fronts of Saxon houses. They were intended to let in a little light, as well as giving much needed extra ventilation in the small, smokey houses.

Knucker Holes.

There were reputed to be four Knucker Dragon holes in West Sussex, which was the only place where the Knucker Dragon was said to live.

They were apparently to be found in Lancing, Shoreham, Lyminster and Worthing, though of the four, only two Knucker Holes still remain. One is to be found on private land near the hamlet of Lyminster, not far from Littlehampton (Hamm Tun), and the other is on Sompting Estate's Church Farm, and this one was restored in 2014.

The word Knucker itself, is said to come from the old Saxon word Nicor, which meant "water monster" and is mentioned in the great poem Beowulf.

The Wildwood.

Known in Roman times as Anderida, and in later Saxon and Medieval times as The Weald. It was an almost impenetrable forest which spread from Romney Marsh, Kent in the East, to what is now the New Forest in Hampshire over in the West. This would have been an area which covered some 120 miles or more wide and as much as 30 miles deep, stretching from the South Coast right up to the outskirts of London.

Although the Romans had created passages, or droves through parts of the forest, the vast majority remained completely wild and contained wild boar and wolves, and some think that even the last few bears in England may have lived within it.

After the Saxons invaded England, killing or driving the *Welsh/Wealsc* (Britons) from their homes, some fled into the Weald and created new settlements deep within it and far away from their enemies. Many of these settlements still exist, although now of course, they have of grown into villages and towns over the years.

Right up until the late Middle Ages, the forest was still a dangerous area as it was a known hiding place for highwaymen, bandits and all manner of outlaws.

Coming soon.......

Book Two

Drefan and the Green Man.©

from

email: renweardpress@yahoo.com

Made in the USA
Columbia, SC
10 November 2017